# THE BEAUTIFUL YEARS

## KATIA LIEF

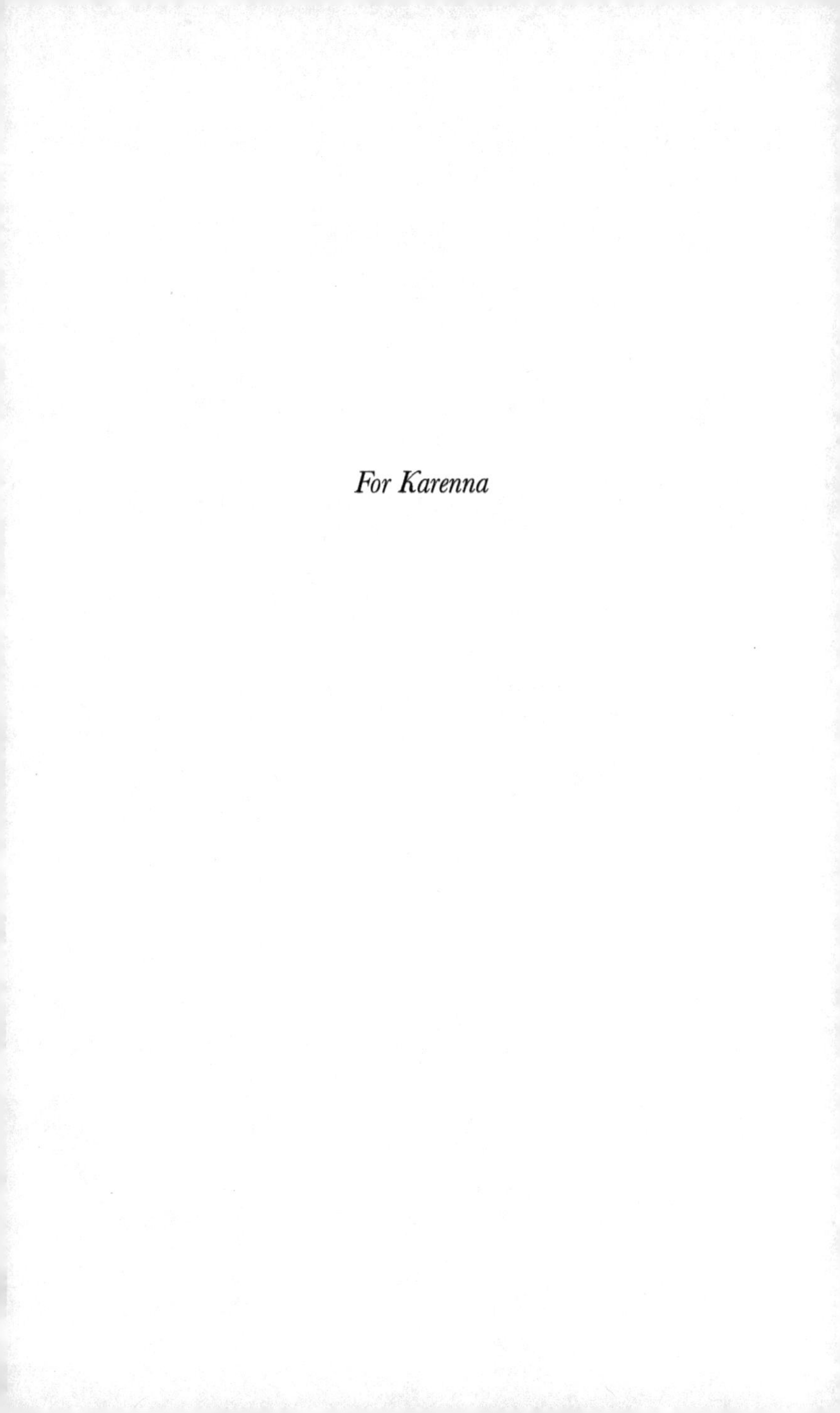

*For Karenna*

# THE BEAUTIFUL YEARS

## ❧ I ❧

## ENDING

A white tent had been installed yesterday on the Great Lawn, and overnight a stage and podium had appeared. Ada could see it from her dorm room: the broad slab of shadow trembling on the freshly mowed grass, the warm blue morning, the buzz of preparations for graduation that afternoon.

George was fast asleep in her single bed, hogging most of it, as usual. He slept with his mouth slack, drool collected in one corner. She sat on the edge of the mattress and raked her fingers through his hair, thick, sandy, always with a faint smell of chlorine from not shampooing after swim team practice. How she had managed to couple up with practically the only engineering major at a liberal arts college continued to amaze her. But George had a lot of imagination, and he was sweet. She used the edge of the sheet to wipe the dribble off his lips, and then lightly slapped his cheek. A blush appeared on his skin, and she felt a little guilty. His eyes began to flutter open.

"It's time," she said. "Let's go wake up Claude."

Heat stung George's cheek, creating a sudden plunge out of a dream flight that had had him soaring twenty feet above the ground, held aloft by a magic elixir of willpower, competence and grace. Now he was falling, the ground was opening, there was a chasm of darkness, he felt afraid, and his face hurt. His eyes cracked open to the reality of Ada, naked from the waist up, staring at him. He was always happy to see Ada, and he forgave her the surprise awakening.

He groaned, "What?"

"Time to dig up the time capsule. Come on."

George remembered, and sat up. Four years ago, during freshman orientation week, he, Ada and Claude had become fast friends. One night they'd decided to bury a bunch of random stuff in a time capsule, to be excavated when they graduated. At the time, none of them had believed that day would ever come. They'd been stoned, and now he couldn't remember everything they'd put in there. They'd filled a small plastic container and buried it under a tree at the bottom of campus near Bates cafeteria.

The mess of boxes in Ada's dorm room reminded him that, in a matter of hours, they'd all be gone. His own room, where he rarely slept, was already packed up. He wondered if Claude had made any headway at all; as of last night, he hadn't even built his boxes. George reached behind Ada's neck to pull her in for a kiss, maybe more, but she laughed, stood up and said, "Get dressed."

He swung his legs to the floor and pulled on the jeans he'd left puddled beside the bed. He smelled yesterday's T-shirt to make sure it wasn't too rank, and pulled it on. Ada meanwhile put on a clean white T, without a bra, and stood waiting for him in her tight jeans and sneakers while he brushed his teeth in her bathroom. When he came out and saw her—hands jammed into back pockets, a shadow of nipple visible under white cotton—her casual beauty took him by surprise. Which, in and of itself, was not a surprise, as this kind of tiny revelation tended to bubble through his days.

Ada loved the way George was looking at her, the way his eyes squinted a little. She loved him. "Let's grab some coffee." Her brain felt murky, and the Pub was on the way to Slonim Woods. She'd thought of living with them there—the townhouse residences tucked into the woods were coed—but was glad she'd chosen to stay in her room in MacCracken. It was central, smack in the middle of campus, which she liked. She'd also worried that living with her two best friends, one of whom she was sleeping with, could get claustrophobic. And what if she and George ever broke up? Not that they would, but anything was possible.

Her sophomore poetry teacher, Tom, long blond hair tucked behind his ears, high-fived her when they crossed paths on the Great Lawn, by the edge of the tent. "Congrats, Ada! What's next for you?"

"I've got a summer internship lined up at Random House," she said. Fingers crossed it turns into a real job."

He literally crossed his fingers, and showed her, which made her want to laugh. But he was a good teacher and she liked him, so she didn't. "Thanks."

"What about you, George?" Tom asked.

George had never studied with Tom, who was a renowned poet along with being a tenured professor here at the college, but he knew him thanks to Ada. "I've got a paying gig at Google, in Manhattan. I start on Monday, actually."

Tom's eyebrows shot up. "Awesome. Really awesome." George had found that the artsy adults he told about his new job were generally impressed with, and maybe a little jealous of, the potential solidity of his career path. Artsy kids, on the other hand—nearly all the other students here at school—tended to react with suspicion. But George was excited, really excited, to start this new phase of his life. They were paying him a hundred grand, plus a fifteen thousand dollar signing bonus, and he could expect a fifteen percent performance bonus if things went well. There would also be stock shares over time, and other "soft" benefits, as the Human Resources woman had described the many daily perks of working at a place with things like pool tables and unlimited free food. The office was in Chelsea, and he'd be able to afford an apartment nearby if that's where he and Ada decided to live. So far, she kept talking about Brooklyn. They'd agreed to put off the decision until after graduation, and meantime stay with Claude at his parents' penthouse on Sutton Place while the folks summered in the Hamptons. George's parents had offered to put them up in his childhood apartment in Queens, but they'd preferred to stay in Manhattan. Ada was from Rhode Island, and at some point they would visit her family for a long weekend, maybe two, but otherwise they'd roost in the city and get their lives started right away.

Glen Washington Road was unusually busy with cars entering the large visitors' lot, even though it was still hours to graduation. A steady stream of parental vehicles turned off Kimball Avenue onto campus—probably, Ada figured, to get a jump on packing the car before the ceremony. Underclassmen had moved out yesterday, to lessen the havoc. Ada had felt an unexpected sadness watching them go, aware that she would never see most of them again. That was when it really hit her that a major part of her life was over: when the younger students kept telling each other, "See you in the fall!" and Ada knew she wouldn't.

They trudged across campus to Slonim Woods. Ada finished her coffee halfway across Kimball and handed her cardboard cup to George. He took it without complaint and nested his inside hers in a way that made her wish she'd walked her empty over to the trash can herself. Why did he never question her? She'd noticed that only when Claude pointed it out to her one day, a few months ago, when she'd demanded to know why he'd rolled his eyes.

"You're not very nice to him sometimes," Claude had said. It was night, and they were sitting on a bench outside the Pub. George had gone inside to the bathroom, and Ada watched the door in case he came back and heard them talking. In daylight Claude's eyes were often bloodshot, a ghoulishly patriotic red-white-and-blue, but at night they shone silver-bright in the darkness. Ada inched closer, making sure not to touch him.

She asked, "What do you mean?"

"Seriously?"

"I'm nice to him."

"You kind of push him around. He does whatever you want, and he never argues."

"He'd tell me if he wasn't happy."

Claude snorted in a way that felt judgmental to Ada. What did he know about relationships? Claude was ridiculously handsome and had slept with half the girls on campus, but he'd never had a real girlfriend.

After that, Ada started to notice how right Claude was. She began to adjust her behavior, to polish off the hard edges, as her mother might have said.

George opened Slonim's front door for Ada, who sighed and went in. She seemed upset about something. "You okay?" he asked. He tried again, "What's wrong?"

"Nothing. Just, you know, today."

George knew that Ada could be sensitive and moody. Personally, he was excited about the changes coming their way; but at the same time, he could understand why she might feel nervous. Graduating from college was a huge deal— George was only the second person in his family to do so. Moving into the city was also big. And starting a career. He pictured her sitting by a sunny window in their new place, writing poetry.

True to form, Claude had fallen asleep on top of his covers, wearing what they called his "Pollock" jeans because they were covered in paint and he never washed them. He must have stayed late in Heimbold last night, working in his studio, instead of packing up like he'd said he planned to do. His room was its usual mess. A thick stack of cardboard boxes leaned flattened against a wall, their seams unbroken.

George laughed and said, "Dude!"

Claude didn't move. He was lithe and pale and dark-haired, with thick eyebrows and a pronounced Adam's apple that Ada had a sudden desire to lick. She leaned close to his ear and said, "Wake up!" He smelled like weed.

His bright blue eyes snapped open and fixed on her, hovering inches from his face. His lashes were long and tender as a baby's. His lips gathered the way they did just before he told someone to fuck off, but instead he thrust his face forward and kissed her hard on the lips. Shocked, she stood up. As she knew he would, George came to her rescue.

"What was that?"

"She shouted in my ear." Claude curled to the side, yawned, and slowly came to sitting.

"You don't kiss my girl," George said, but he was laughing a little, which bothered Ada. It wasn't funny. It was aggressive of Claude to kiss her like that, especially in front of George—provocative, to both of them. But, on the other hand, Claude was being Claude. He crossed boundaries and broke rules as if he had invented the concept. Sometimes she resented him because of it, but it wasn't really resentment, it was something else that she couldn't quite put her finger on.

George hoped he'd made his point without being overly dramatic. He didn't want to start any trouble, given that they were all moving into Claude's parents' penthouse that night. Claude was a monster before morning coffee. George still had a few inches left in his cup, so he handed it over and Claude finished it in one long sip.

Claude put the empty cup on the floor and noticed that it was doubled into another one. He looked at his friends and said, "Time capsule —let's go!"

They ran across campus, laughing, all three holding hands, making people swerve around them. At the bottom of the hill, Ada and Claude slowed down to catch their breath. George could have kept running, but he waited for them. He wished this could go on forever, he loved them both so much, loved the three of them together. Later, looking back, he'd recognize this as their last perfect moment.

They walked the rest of the way down the path, stepped over a short scalloped iron fence, and found their tree. In reality, it was smaller and grayer, its branches skimpier, than in his mind when, over the years, he'd recalled the night they buried the time capsule.

Claude stood with his back against the trunk, where a root humped over the ground, and repeated what they'd all memorized four years ago. "Six feet in the direction of Bates's southeast corner." Using his shoes as measures, he walked heel-to-toe six steps forward.

Ada used the edge of her sneaker to push away a thin coating of leaves above the spot. She was afraid—and excited. She vaguely remembered writing something and sealing it in an envelope, something that she knew might embarrass her, but she couldn't remember what, or about whom.

"We're idiots," George said, wishing he'd been more on the ball. He knew by now that relying on either one of them was a gamble; they were artists, dreamy, and he sometimes thought that without him they might float away. "We didn't think to bring something to dig with."

Ada said, "Oh, no."

"Fuck it." Claude pulled his iPhone out of the back pocket of his jeans, popped off the hand-crafted wood case, fell to his knees, and began to scrape away at the earth.

"You spent like—" George stopped himself from completing his sentence: fifty bucks on that thing. He recalled the day Claude had bought it, handing over his credit card (his parents' credit card) without a second thought, at a twee gift shop in Williamsburg. He already had a perfectly good phone case, but this one had caught his eye. George had mostly learned to stifle himself when it came to the Fisher family wealth, the noxious pellets of his friend's purchases swallowed and forgotten. Now, watching Claude dig and dig with the pretty case, dirt stained, edges splintering, George's gift-shop thought bubbled back: he would never waste his money on something like that; he wouldn't replace something if it wasn't necessary; he would search online for the best deal. But he wasn't Claude, who George recognized had every right to live the life he was dealt.

Claude rapped the dirt-encrusted phone case against something hard. "Got it!"

"We didn't bury it very deeply," George said, crouching down. Ada knelt beside him and gently touched his back, igniting a familiar tremor of warmth.

Claude reached down to retrieve the box. The once translucent plastic had grown cloudy and cracked, but the seal hadn't broken. George used his bare hands to push the displaced dirt back into the hole before someone from Grounds caught wind of what they were doing. Ada stamped the dirt back into place. Claude, meanwhile, started to peel off the dry, cruddy tape.

George stopped him. "Not here."

"He's right," Ada agreed. "Let's take it to my room."

They walked back up the path toward MacCracken. Claude carried the box, enjoying the smell of musty earth it emanated after four years underground. It was a seductive idea—that kind of hibernation, disappearance, secrecy, privacy, invisibility. Sometimes he wished he could vanish so completely, be known only to a few important people to whom he actually mattered—George and Ada, definitely; his parents, maybe. He got his best ideas when he was alone, deeply alone, a visceral yearning for which led his thoughts back to the painting he'd worked on late into last night. The world quieted exponentially when everyone else was asleep. Darkness thickened. Inspiration flowed. And if he got high, it was ever better. He wondered if he could find time, even half an hour, to get back to the studio before graduation. Getting dressed wouldn't take him long. He could skip a shower.

On their way up the hill, they passed a cluster of well-dressed family members surrounding a classmate who had already donned her cap and gown. It made Ada nervous: their delight as they made their way in the direction of the tent and presumably the choicest seats. She tended to distrust people who lined up extremely early for best access. But then she thought of her parents and younger sister, on their way down from Rhode Island, and wondered if she ought to save them seats in advance. And then hated herself for thinking that. Her youth was about to end. Why couldn't she live in the moment?

She pushed open the door to MacCracken so hard it bashed against the wall, saying, "I have to pee." The moment the three got inside, she disappeared into her bathroom.

The bed was still unmade. Claude sat on the rumpled sheet, still damp from George, who tended to sweat at night. George stood there, watching his friend drum his fingertips atop the plastic box. Claude wore a thick silver ring on his left forefinger, and his nails were edged with dirt.

George leaned in and whispered, "I'm asking her to marry me tonight."

Claude froze, a blossom of cold emanating from his stomach. "Why?"

"That's a funny question."

"Why didn't you tell me?"

"I'm telling you now."

"When did you decide?"

"Will you be my best man?"

"What if she doesn't say yes?"

George laughed. Just at that moment, the toilet flushed, and Ada emerged, wiping her damp hands on the front of her jeans. "What's so funny?" By the look on George's face, Claude must have told a joke. He rarely told jokes, and so she wanted to hear it.

But George said, "Nothing."

Claude's expression clouded with something

that definitely wasn't humor. Ada felt a prickle crawl along her spine. She rubbed the base of her neck until the uncomfortable sensation was gone.

She sat down beside Claude, took the box off his lap, and ripped off the tape. It took a moment to pry the top loose. A musky smell sprang from within, like opening a grandmother's closet. She picked up an orange plastic thumb drive. "Whose was this?"

"Mine." Claude smiled, remembering. "It's got all my high school homework."

Ada's hand thrust into the box, digging for something halfway in. "Here it is!" It was a Justin Bieber CD she'd stolen from her little sister when she was packing for college, to help wean Lori off the teen idol and prove her far superior taste. At that point, Ada had just discovered Billie Holiday. "Lori went ballistic when she couldn't find this."

Ada then plucked out a glass vacuum tube, a ring of prongs like little legs at one end. "We know who this belongs to." She smiled and handed it to George. The cold, smooth glass nestled in the palm of his hand. He'd been an audio purist in high school, obsessed with analog technology. Ada, hardly knowing him in those early days four years ago, had challenged him to bury one of his "weird plugs." He'd offered up one of his best tubes, hoping to impress her, though she obviously couldn't tell the difference.

There were items they'd nearly forgotten: Ada's frequent-buyer punch card from a Rhode Island café, now closed; George's single white sock; Claude's five dollar bill on which he had drawn a smiley face over Abraham Lincoln. And others that surfaced with visceral flashes: Ada's red wristband stamped you are the 99%, the sight of which rekindled a sensation of clear purpose she had rarely felt since; George's first girlfriend's final gift to him, a magnetized blue pom-pom with a pair of googly eyes glued on; Claude's high school graduation bow tie, a sartorial error the internet would never let him live down. Foraging through the items deposited by selves they'd hoped to leave behind, they saved the letters for last.

There were three identical envelopes, each unmarked. Ada chose one at random and ripped it open. She read aloud:

"The minute I saw you I knew that you were going to be the one. Do you feel the same way?"

It was her own handwriting, and she

pretended not to recognize it. She was grateful beyond belief that she hadn't used names.

George read the next one, recognizing the jagged shapes of Claude's handwriting. "Fun night. Great music. Who wants to watch Beetlejuice?"

They all laughed. Ada couldn't be sure which one of the boys might have written the note. It had been a fun night. They all loved music. Of the three of them, she was the only one who hadn't arrived at school obsessed with that crazy movie.

At eighteen, Claude had been mostly unable to articulate himself. Given the chance to write his note again, now, he would have taken more of a risk. Hearing his inane words made him recall what had really gone through his mind that night, pen in hand. He'd been intensely attracted to Ada, so much so that he'd been unable to look her in the eye. He handed the remaining unopened envelope to George.

George read the final letter, smiling at its prescience. "I just met the girl I'm going to marry someday."

Ada's jaws slung open. Her eyes flit to Claude,

and then to George, who was smiling. She closed her lips and smiled back. How had he known right away? She herself had been attracted to both of them, but more strongly to Claude. It was only over time, as she got to know them well, that George's good character and perseverance had won out. Claude had been promiscuous almost right away, and it had bothered her. When he'd tried to invite himself into her room late one night, early on, she'd turned him down, thinking that she didn't want to be just one of his conquests; he'd have to work harder for her. But he never tried again.

"We should probably think about getting changed," Ada said. "Our parents will start showing up soon."

Claude overturned the time capsule onto Ada's bed and riffled his hand through the random stuff, searching for an unearthed surprise. "We didn't have much imagination when we were eighteen, did we?"

"We thought we did." Ada smiled at Claude; she felt the same way: disappointed. She didn't know what she'd expected. Maybe that their former selves had known something that the box would reveal. She wasn't sure. "Who knows, maybe four years from now we'll look back at today and think the same thing."

"We were young," George said, "not stupid. Ada's right, we should start getting ready." His parents tended to be punctual; they'd be arriving in half an hour.

"Yeah, but," Claude stood abruptly, "the question is: Get ready for what?" In a way, the fact that his parents would be willing, unasked, to support him in his career as an artist felt like a kind of death sentence. This wasn't something he felt he could say aloud to his friends, both of whom expected to work for a living. For Claude, working for a living was optional, and that he could decide, actually decide, terrified him. People who didn't have money always thought that wealth was a panacea, but it wasn't. It was a crucible. Both his parents had inherited fortunes, and neither had had a talent or calling. They worked on boards. Volunteered. Traveled. Collected art. They had named him after Claude Monet because they aspired to own one, and eventually did. Now that painting on the living room wall felt like a taunt: With nothing but time and opportunity, Claude Fisher's talent had better be real.

"Chill," George advised, expertly reading his friend's mood. He could tell by now, in the twitch of Claude's movements, when anxiety was surfacing. "It's just a ceremony. It's just one day. Put on your suit and get through it."

"That's another thing," Claude said. "Why wear a suit when it'll be hidden under the gown, anyway?"

Ada agreed. "That's a good point. But still, if I don't wear a dress under my gown, my mother will make a thing, and I'm not going there."

George opened the door and waited for Claude to pass into the hall. He looked at Ada, standing in her room of boxes, each one labeled with its contents. Her striped graduation dress hung on the front of the closet door, patent leather sandals propped on the floor beneath. As usual, she was more prepared than she tended to give herself credit for. A worrier, she strategized and organized everything in advance, and then pretended to be more carefree than she actually was. It was one of the contradictions he loved about her. "See you under the tent," he said.

"Twenty minutes," Ada answered, thinking: wash face, brush teeth, makeup, dress, jewelry, shoes. She liked to factor in extra time in case the outfit wasn't working. "Half an hour, at the most."

Claude walked down the hall, pulled open the outer door and felt the whoosh of spring air and the coil of panic tighten. His parents would be late, but even if they were on time, it wouldn't matter. He could go to his studio before changing and pull his head together.

"You didn't get your suit cleaned," George asked him, "did you?"

"It's clean already."

"I thought I saw it on your closet floor last week."

"Good. Then I won't have to search."

"Maybe don't bother with the suit." George thought that, on balance, it would be worse for Claude to wear the crumpled, dirty suit than fresh jeans and a T-shirt. It was a matter of degree and overall impact.

"Listen—"

Claude's tone gave George a sudden, bad feeling. This was how his friend sounded when he'd made up his mind about something: clipped, inflexible. Anxious. Often, that was when things spun out of control, but this was not a good time for an emotional bender. They needed to get through the day. For now, that was all. Later, Claude could visit his demons all he wanted. Maybe demons wasn't the right word. Neither was passion, or inspiration. Craving was more like it. Claude craved elusive satisfactions, and he chased after them, hard. George had stopped letting Claude's wild flights scare him the way they used to; now, he waited, and they always passed.

"—I'm going to head to the studio for a bit," Claude finished his sentence. He didn't look at George, because he didn't want any feedback. He was doing it. It was happening.

They walked toward Slonim Woods in silence, George's hands jammed into his front pockets, Claude's arms swinging loose at his sides. From time to time, Claude stretched out his fingers so the damp skin of his palms could dry. It was hard to breathe. As soon as Heimbold came into view, square and glassy in the near distance, he broke into a jog and left his friend behind.

George watched Claude put enough distance between them that anyone who saw them from afar wouldn't think they'd been together. It was just as well. Now George would be able to get dressed quickly and return to the tent to await his family. Claude's reaction to George's announcement about his intentions for Ada had stung, and being alone for a little while would allow him to realign his confidence.

Ada stood at the window of her dorm room, which smelled like cardboard from all the boxes. She both hated and loved the smell, because it meant change, and she both hated and loved change. It terrified her, and yet she wanted it.

She felt the minutes ticking forward, a minor thumping in her chest. She watched George and Claude cross the Great Lawn, veering away from the tent and the thin crowd beginning to gather. They moved in synch with each other, their gaits undulating like sleepy cats. Though she couldn't be sure, it seemed to her, from the way their heads didn't turn, that they had stopped talking. George had put his hands in his pockets, which was a form of punctuation she recognized as his bid for silence. And then, suddenly, Claude took off running, his dark hair rising and falling on a self-generated breeze.

She thought of something Claude had told them that his father said to his mother on their honeymoon: "I knew when I met you that you would be my third wife." There was a twenty-year age difference, and they'd met when he was on the verge of marrying Mrs. Fisher number two. Their family was unlike any that Ada had ever known. Poor Claude—she could hardly imagine what he'd been up against, all his life, with parents like that. And the strange older half brothers, who never, ever called.

At the far edge of the tent, she saw Missy Baldwin, George's mother, appear and then immediately disappear into a thick shadow. Harry Baldwin couldn't be too far behind. She wondered if George's brother and sister, John and Ellen, had come along. Of course they had, she thought, a moment before the little boy came skipping into view. Ellen appeared next, looking like a proven adult, a year after her own college graduation, the way she strode unselfconsciously forward to join her mother in the shadow's oblivion. Of course they were all here, together. They were that kind of family.

Ada felt queasy all of a sudden and sat on the edge of her bed until it passed.

George's smell rose from the sheets. She breathed it in.

She stripped naked and lifted her arms into

the dress, like a double salute, and closed her eyes while the soft fabric enveloped her.

Claude loved the smell of oil paint when it was freshly laid onto a canvas, and he loved it even more when it had dried in strands of unintentional abstraction on the floor. He was the only one left in the studio; everyone else had packed up and vacated. White rectangles floated on the paint-splattered walls where frameless canvases had been pulled down, stark edges of color reinforcing the concept of empty space.

He didn't want to be alone here. He'd been wrong; this was a mistake.

He didn't want any of this to end, that was the thing. These had been the best four years of his life. The moment he and George and Ada stepped into his parents' penthouse later tonight would mark the beginning of the end. For them, it would be the first step toward leaving each other. George and Ada would find their own place, move on, and he would be…nowhere.

He dropped his brush—acid-orange splashing onto the adjacent wall—walked to the corner and unstacked a pyramid of empty paint cans. He held the bottom can between his knees—rivulets of dry green paint fringing the sides—and used a key to pry open the lid. The plastic Rite Aid bag was exactly where he'd left it, twisted at the bottom of the can.

He unknotted the bag, took out the balled-up pillowcase and spread it on the floor. Then he laid out his works, one piece at a time. Adrenaline hissed and bubbled even before he held the spoon of powder above the lighter's shivering flame. He watched, closely, as the heroin turned to liquid.

Claude sat back against the wall and pushed up his sleeve. Using his teeth he tightened the rubber tourniquet around his upper arm, and tapped for a vein in the crease of his elbow. He still had good veins in his arm, he hadn't blown them yet; the minute he had to move on to other body parts was when he'd quit. The foreshadowing of pleasure was so intense that the prick of breaking skin no longer hurt. The needle slid in easily. Hunching over his arm, he watched it thread into the vein.

Ada opened her arms, but Lori stood back. Somehow, her little sister had convinced their parents to let her wear jeans and flip-flops. She had a fresh pedicure, blue; that was something. Their mother hugged Ada tightly, taking the opportunity to whisper, "She's depressed. We didn't want to push."

"Good call," Ada whispered back. She knew from visits home and frequent phone calls that puberty had hit Lori hard. It ran in the family. Ada herself had been there, and antidepressants had helped her over the hump. When her mother released her, she rose onto her toes to kiss her father's freshly shaven cheek. He'd had a haircut and was wearing his best suit, and Ada felt proud. Her mother had cleaned an old dress, a lavender one Ada once coveted, and she'd colored the gray out of her short hair. Philip and Diana Green were both elementary school teachers, and despite the generous financial aid Ada had been given by the school, her tuition had still been a stretch. If her internship didn't pan out with something permanent by the end of the summer, she'd have to find a real job, anything that paid. George had hinted that she could take her time, but it felt retro to count on him financially. No. She wouldn't do it.

As if her mother could read her thoughts, Diana asked, "Where's George?"

Ada pointed across the lawn, where the Baldwins were taking turns photographing each other surrounding their graduate. He was wearing his cap and gown, the blue fabric fluttering. He looked happy. She smiled while her parents waved at him, but George didn't appear to notice them.

"And Claude?" Philip asked. Ada, George and Claude had taken turns staying with each other's families over the past three Thanksgivings, and now each set of parents seemed to feel a proprietary affection for their child's close friends.

Ada moved her gaze across the growing crowd. "I don't see him." Or his parents, an observation that rankled.

Lori was wrapping a strand of hair around and around her finger. Diana looked at Ada and sighed. "Any place we can grab a quick bite before the ceremony?" Mouthing silently: Lori hasn't eaten anything today.

"The Pub."

They knew where it was.

"I'll save you seats," Ada called after them.

"Thanks, honey." Philip turned around with a wink and then followed Diana and Lori into the Pub. Ada wondered why he had to go with them, but it wasn't worth asking. They lived with Lori full time, she didn't, which on balance was a real relief.

Ada made her way under the tent and found three unclaimed seats together. She draped her gown over two and put her cap on the third. It was cooler under the tent, a little chilly actually, and she made her way back into the sun, in the direction of George and his family.

George saw Ada crossing the lawn toward him, rubbing her bare arms. She looked gorgeous in the striped dress. It was lower cut than she normally wore, accentuating the sensual bosom she tended to hide. Her skin had a soft, golden hue from the past few weeks of sunshine. She had put on some makeup, but she didn't need it; in fact, he preferred her without.

Last night, lying together in her bed, she'd recited a poem by Sara Teasdale:

> *When I went to look at what had long*
> *    been hidden,*
> *A jewel laid long ago in a secret place,*

*I trembled, for I thought to see its dark
    deep fire,
But only a pinch of dust blew up in my
    face.*

*I almost gave my life long ago for a
    thing
That has gone to dust now, stinging my
    eyes,
It is strange how often a heart must be
    broken,
Before the years can make it wise.*

"It's called 'Dust,'" Ada had said.

George had repeated, "Dust," not knowing what else to say. He'd found that he needed to read a poem several times to get its meaning, if he did at all. And he'd never even heard of Sara Teasdale.

She asked, "What did you think of it?"

"It's nice."

She turned on him, tickling him under the arms until he lost control laughing. They ended up making love. After, lying side by side, staring up at the over-painted white ceiling, she repeated, "When I went to look at what had long been hidden…only a pinch of dust blew up in my face."

He'd listened to the words float up to the ceiling and pop into nothingness like lost balloons.

Only now, watching her move toward him across the lawn, waving at his family, did he finally understand. It was about the time capsule, as if she'd known in advance that the leavings of their teenage selves wouldn't be particularly revealing. The Beetlejuice thing—that was obviously Claude. And the note about how attracted Ada was to George from the very beginning had only told him what he already knew. "Only a pinch of dust blew up in my face." It was a reminder, to George, to live in the moment. Like Ada walking toward him, right now, on a warm spring day, surrounded by his family. The only thing that would make it more perfect was if Claude were standing beside him.

Walking toward George and his family, Ada kept thinking about Claude. Worrying, really. And, to be honest, also feeling a little pissed. Why wasn't he here with them now, ready for the ceremony? Why did his moods have to complicate things? She chastised herself for thinking that. It was a hard day for all of them.

After exchanging hugs and kisses with every member of George's family, she wove her arm through his and stood there enduring the eager gaze of his mother. It was an open secret that Missy Baldwin adored Ada, which made Ada feel that she was bound to disappoint eventually. Finally, George leaned to her ear and asked, softly, "Where's Claude?"

George and Ada shared a meaningful glance. Obviously, Claude was hiding out in his studio. Just as obviously, George was stuck here with his family. Ada said, "I'll go find him."

George called after her, "His suit is—" on his closet floor, but she cut him off with a dismissive wave of her hand. Ada was right. It didn't matter what Claude wore under his gown; at this point, it only mattered that he made it to the lawn in the next forty-five minutes.

Ada's steps echoed on Heimbold's polished concrete floor. They'd gone all out when they'd built the arts center; only the best for the country's most expensive school. Five years ago, it was her dream to come here, so she could do this, now: stride through the glass building, about to graduate and begin the rest of her life. She slowed down. Other than Claude, who presumably was still in his studio, she was the only one in the building. The slap of each of her footsteps resounded through the space like a newly formed word aching with meaning but yet to be defined.

She pushed open the studio door, and there was Claude, sprawled on the floor in the far corner, beside a jumble of old paint cans. Her heart leaped; for a second, she thought he was dead. But then his head turned and he pushed himself up onto his elbows to look at her. His eyes were glassy; it seemed he'd been crying. She hurried to him.

Claude opened his eyes and there was Ada, dreamlike, approaching through a swirl of color. It was the most beautiful thing he'd ever seen. He had loved her forever. And now, just before everything was about to end, here she was.

He looked so pale, and as she got closer she realized how vulnerable he was. Beneath the talent, the neuroses, the swagger, the handsomeness, the trail of other girls, there was a needy boy. She felt a powerful desire to hold him in her arms.

She had long felt this, but now it was over-whelming.

Ada fell to her knees, as if he'd dreamed it, and pulled him up off the floor. She smelled like ripe berries. He closed his eyes and allowed himself to kiss the underside of her chin.

She felt Claude's kiss, and for a moment confusion rose. But no. No. This time she wouldn't let the possibility vanish. She angled her face above his. Their mouths, an inch apart. She had once dreamed that Claude's lips gently kissed the palm of her hand, and had woken up to find George beside her. Worse, she'd reached between George's legs and they'd made love furiously.

Claude's tongue found its way into her mouth, and she was on her knees, and he was lying back against the floor, and she felt that she could eat him whole.

Her mouth felt just as Claude had always imagined it, soft and giving, warm. Shades of bright yellow exploded through him.

Ada sucked at him, wanting more. He seemed different somehow, supplicant, and as his hand gently traveled under her dress and onto her bottom, she wondered if he was high. But he didn't smell like weed. And she didn't care.

The sensation was new for Claude: it was like drowning and swimming at the same time. He couldn't count how many girls he'd fucked, but with Ada it was completely different. So this was what making love was. Gold, spilled light.

Ada scratched at his zipper. His erection was long and hard under the front of his jeans. She was wet, her underpants were soaked, and when he tried to pull them off she helped him. But the fabric around his zipper was too tight and she couldn't pull it down. Finally, his hand found hers. For a moment, he wove his fingers through hers and they lay there, panting, held-hands crushed between them.

If Claude had a single wish, and he could make it right now, in this state of high impairment, it would be to remain like this forever.

Suddenly, his zipper was down, and her hand was in his underwear. His penis was longer and thinner than George's, but harder, she thought; she wasn't sure. She pushed her other hand against the floor to create a separation between their bodies, opened her legs, let him find her, and in one hard thrust they entered each other.

Ada gasped.

Claude's mind exploded: blankness; pure white.

They found a rhythm together, fast, and then by unspoken mutual agreement slowed to a lullaby. "It was for you," she said, whispering, "what I wrote in the time capsule."

The minute I saw you I knew that you were going to be the one. Do you feel the same way?

Claude reached behind her to unzip her dress. It fell to her waist and he put his hands on her breasts, and he said, finally said it, said it out loud: "I fucking love you, Ada."

"Me, too."

Ada's body convulsed in rhythm with Claude's. She collapsed on top of him, thought of George, and wept.

## 2

# MIDDLE

Claudia ran ahead along Madison Avenue, the bottom of her new navy dress dipping below the hem of a winter coat she had outgrown. The backs of her new patent shoes popped off with every step; they would fit six months from now, when she no longer needed them. Ada walked behind her, prepared to shout "Stop!" when her daughter reached the corner. At almost five, Claudia was pretty good about not darting into traffic, but you never knew.

As it turned out, a reminder wasn't needed. At the corner, Ada reached down, and Claudia offered up her little hand. They crossed 79th Street in a tide of well-heeled Upper East Siders.

The pavement actually sparkled here on a sunny day—a far cry from the garbage-strewn sidewalks of Bushwick where they'd paid an increasingly exorbitant rent for a large but shoddy loft. They had built a separate room in a far back corner for Claudia. A room with a door, walls painted pink, a mobile handmade by Claude dangling from the center of the ceiling. Shelves of books and toys and stuffed animals, everywhere. Ada wondered if the Fishers would continue to pay the rent, now, and forcefully pushed the subject out of her mind. It was going to be a very difficult day, and her only goal at the moment was to get through it.

A long black hearse was parked in front of the Frank E. Campbell Funeral Chapel. People were beginning to arrive, dressed mournfully and in good taste. Claude would have hated this. He'd only ever owned the one suit, and she'd never seen him wear it. A yellow taxi pulled to a stop behind the hearse, and Jeffrey Fisher, one of Claude's older half brothers, emerged behind a young woman Ada had never seen before. Blonde, blow-dried, high-heeled, the whole bit. Jeffrey's head hung—sad or ashamed, Ada couldn't tell from a distance—as he crossed into the funeral home. She wondered if her own parents had arrived yet; they had insisted on coming, even though she'd begged them not to.

Claudia waited for her mother in front of the building where everyone was going in. People she recognized. She wished her mother wouldn't be so slow. Her father was faster, funner, and for a moment she wondered when he would get here, and then remembered that he wouldn't. Or maybe he was already here. Her mother had explained it all to her before, but it was still fuzzy. Basically, it had made no sense at all when her mother said that she would only ever see her father again in memories and dreams.

Ada held open the heavy door for Claudia, who raced in, straight to her grandparents. Harry and Christina Fisher, for once sober and on time, stood just inside the entrance greeting guests. Christina, haggard, beautifully dressed, crouched down to hug Claudia, and Ada heard her daughter say, "I don't like this, Nanna."

Christina answered, "Neither do I," her voice dry and weak.

Ada pecked Christina's cheek. Christina patted Ada lightly on the back.

About twenty people were already there, and Ada didn't expect many more. There were family and friends, but as Claude had never formally worked, there were no colleagues. Though she did note the presence of the owner of a Chelsea gallery that had signed Claude on last year and then waited for a show that never jelled. Now, the owner, whose name was Jacka Tornado—a ridiculous name that couldn't be real but that Claude had informed Ada was—spotted Ada entering. Jacka nodded, just a little, and Ada nodded back, just a little. Ada was grateful for the constant distractions provided by Claudia, who had flung her coat onto the nearest chair. Ada intercepted it just as it slid toward the floor.

Neal Fisher, the oldest of the older half brothers, stood by himself in front of a cold fireplace. He held a plastic cup of water, and Ada noticed that his hand was shaking. She had always preferred Neal over Jeffrey, though she had never known either very well. She guessed that Neal was close to fifty, a good twenty-three years older than Claude. He'd grown a stomach, and his hair had started to go gray. Childless, and a widower, he seemed cloaked in gloom by the loss of his youngest brother. Ada wondered why she herself didn't feel as morbid as Neal appeared, and decided that grief probably deepened with age.

She was a wreck, yet she knew she'd rebound. Despite everything that had happened—how Claude's death was like someone gouging out one of her eyes, and she couldn't see even a day into her future—she still felt strong. She knew she had a future, and it was a powerful feeling. It wasn't something she'd dare say to anyone, today, but it was true.

"I'm sorry for your loss," Ada said to Neal, and leaned in to kiss his cheek.

"Thank you." He gave her shoulder a warm squeeze. "I'm sorry for you, and for Claudia. Poor kid. Anything you need—"

"We'll be fine."

"Even so, just ask."

"It's hard to believe he's actually in there." Ada couldn't take her eyes off the gleaming walnut coffin, bedecked with white orchids, in front of the leaded window across the chapel. She was going to cry again. Here it came. But no, not now, she wouldn't.

Claude had done this to himself. Maybe not deliberately, but still, he could have not allowed it to happen. Over and over, he might have made that choice.

She heard her mother's voice out in the reception hall, alerting her to the arrival of the rest of the Greens. Claudia was also a Green, as Ada and Claude had never formally married. He hated convention with such a passion that when, during the pregnancy, she'd suggested linking their names with a hyphen for their child, he'd refused. "Just choose one, it doesn't matter," he had said. Ada had decided that Claudia Fisher would get mixed up with Claude Fisher, and so she'd settled on Claudia Fisher Green, with Fisher relegated to the status of a middle name.

The sound of Diana Green's voice made Ada's heart swell. Suddenly she hungered for her mother. She was about to join her parents in the foyer, but Jacka Tornado chose that moment to approach.

Jacka kissed both Ada's cheeks like she was French, which she wasn't, and like they were friends, which they weren't. She was dressed in black from turtleneck to boots, and except for her bright red lipstick, the gallerist might have passed for a slender shadow. Even her hair was black, short and straight, tucked behind her ears in which tiny diamond studs glimmered. "I'm so sorry, Ada," Jacka said.

"Thank you."

"I have to ask—was he making any art before he…"

"Yes, he was." Frantically. High. In the middle of the night.

"If you ever want to show me, well, I'd still be interested."

"I'm not sure if it belongs to me." Ada glanced at Neal, who nodded thoughtfully.

He muttered, "Right, good question."

Ada said, "He was only twenty-seven, it's not like he had a will or anything."

"Of course not," Jacka said.

She handed business cards to Ada and Neal. "I always thought he was incredibly talented. I loved the last work I saw."

Explosions of bright paint webbed like a tapestry over hollow boxes. They had reminded Ada of skinless veiny muscles wrapped tightly over the disappointments of their college time capsule, and she had instantly hated them. But if they did belong to her now, or more likely to Claudia, and if they were worth anything, she'd have to consider Jacka's offer to show them and thus put them up for sale. Again, she pushed out thoughts of money, and livelihood, and rent coming due, to focus only on today. If she could help lay Claude to rest with something that felt actually restful, then maybe it would count as a final gift to him.

"Excuse me," Ada said to Neal and Jacka, "but I think I hear my parents in the front hall. They came all the way from Rhode Island." Claudia was installed on the knee of Jeffrey's new girlfriend, and Ada felt safe leaving her to go and greet Diana and Philip.

Diana and Christina stood face to face like dance partners, having come to a halt, but still clutching each other's hands. It occurred to Ada that these two women, so different from each other in temperament and lifestyle, were now more bound together than ever as co-grand-mothers of the same little girl. They would circle around Claudia now, lift her out of tragedy. For one quick flash Ada resented the presumption that she herself wouldn't be able to rise to the occasion of all her daughter's needs; but just as swiftly came relief to be insulated by this pair of experi-enced mothers. Harry and Philip, meanwhile, were engaged in some kind of grandfatherly chat, hands fisted into the front pockets of their suit pants as if restraining themselves from hitting someone. The only person worth punishing was gone. The man who had done this to all of them, leaving the entire family network in an emotional lurch, was lying motionless in a coffin in the other room.

Ada's eyes welled when Philip strode over to her and wrapped her up in his arms, hunching down to fully envelop her. He whispered, "Shh, baby, it's okay, it's okay," meaning It isn't okay but we're here for you. Ada wept. She sensed her mother's approach first when her perfume grew stronger, and then when she threw her arms around them both and instigated a subtle rocking. Bound together, a small tight boat on an angry sea.

Claudia came into the entry hall and saw her mother with her grandmothers and grandfathers. Some of them were crying, which made Claudia need to cry, too. "Mommy!" She wiggled between her mother's and grandparents' legs to insert herself into their huddle. She felt the way she felt late at night when she woke up and everyone was asleep and she was afraid. And then the terror would grow and grow, like a shadow creeping up her wall until nearly the whole thing was black. When that happened, she'd give herself permission to scream if the shadow erased every speck of light. She would hold her breath and wait, knowing it was about to happen. But it never did. Something would change, a car would pass, or the sun would start to rise, and light would swish across the wall.

One of her uncle's voices said, "The service is about to start," and the adults unclumped around her. Grandma Diana knelt down to give her a big hug, while Nanna Christina waited her turn, and both grandpas stood there staring at her with funny looks on their faces.

Ada's pulse jumped when Neal appeared in the entryway and announced, "The service is about to start." She didn't want the service to start, because it would be another incremental step toward tomorrow, when it would all be over and she'd wake up alone in her and Claude's bed and all this would be true.

Claudia skipped ahead with Neal. Buffeted between her parents, Ada let herself be guided into the chapel. People were seated, and as she came down the aisle, she kept her eyes down so that she wouldn't have to see anyone's face. She felt horribly guilty for having brought everyone here, as if her proximity to Claude these past five years had put her in a unique position to make him well, and she'd failed. She'd tried at first. When nothing worked, she even went to Nar-Anon meetings. Eventually she put her focus on Claudia and earning a living and hoped for the best when it came to Claude. She'd managed to love him, always, but had grown to assume that, one way or another, their relationship wouldn't last. She just wished it hadn't happened like this.

The front row was reserved for family, and Claudia had saved her a seat. Ada sat down and raised her arm so Claudia could snuggle close. Diana sat on Ada's other side, and Philip beside her. The Fishers sat opposite, across the aisle, in the front row, much as the two families might have arranged themselves for a wedding.

Harry Fisher, Claude's father, was the first eulogist to stand at the podium. His voice trembling in a low register, he recalled his youngest son as a boy, recounting his charm, his intelligence, and his abundant artistic gifts. Harry didn't mention Claude's addiction, Ada guessed, because he couldn't bring himself to talk about it, or didn't know how. Addiction required a special emotional vocabulary that even Ada hadn't mastered. It was a journey that led you, provision-less, under a beating sun, to the edge of a canyon.

A childhood friend, Keith, told a story about Claude when they were in middle school together. They'd attended an exclusive private school in Manhattan where they were known as an odd pair because Keith was "as ugly as Claude was handsome." It was an overstatement, surely, because Keith wasn't bad-looking. What he was doing was paying homage to Claude's beauty, maybe because he didn't know how else to remember him. Claude was "moody and quiet," and "all the girls liked him." Keith recalled in particular a day when Claude ignored the group of popular kids in the cafeteria who were urging him to join them, and instead sat with Keith. This was the best moment of Keith's middle school years. Ada glanced at Christina, sobbing across the aisle, at this young man's affirmation of her son's sensitivity.

One of Claude's painting teachers from college was next to speak. Tall, portly, head lush with white hair, he recalled his student's progress over four years as "mercurial" and "astounding" and shared his "certainty that Claude was going to succeed as an artist and possibly already has." Ada bristled at that. What Claude had done was failed—himself, her, his parents, especially Claudia. Only when the pompous man relinquished the podium could Ada begin to breathe again.

Neal shared memories from family holidays, making it clear how much he had not only loved but also liked his late brother. "I never felt a need to judge him," Neal said, "and I'm glad I didn't, because it wouldn't have helped." This was Ada's favorite eulogy, because it was simple and pure, without equivocation.

And then, to Ada's surprise, Jacka Tornado got up to share her take on Claude, whom she called "Claude Fisher" as if he were already a name-brand artist. So this was how it worked, the putting it out there of a name, making its value a foregone conclusion, a posthumous inevitability. He was a "brilliant painter" whose "accomplishments have yet to be recognized," who would be "acknowledged as an important artist," who was "a martyr to his inspiration." Ada started to feel queasy, listening to Jacka. Claude had worked in a junked-up conflagration of agony and rage and lust and delusion and boredom. It had been painful to watch him. Anyone who had seen it would not have envied his state of inspiration, or romanticized either his methods or the art that sprang from it.

The next and final speaker appeared from the very back of the chapel, where he must have come in late. The even tread of his footsteps up the carpeted aisle drew Ada's attention even before she turned around. Solid and fair, George was a man now. She hadn't seen him since graduation, immediately after which she'd confessed that she'd slept with Claude. She remembered, with painful clarity, her exact words and the look on George's face.

"Claude and I made love on the studio floor." No apology. No explanation. Just the fact.

First he laughed, and then his expression buckled into numb disbelief, followed by hurt and then, swiftly, indignation. "I don't believe it," he'd said. "That's insane. Ada, you didn't, did you?"

Now, George, whose eyesight used to be perfect, wore rimless glasses and a well-fitted black suit. Ada's eyes stayed glued to him, and when he passed, just inches away, she felt a current navigate between them. He didn't look at her. When his fingers curled around the edges of the podium, she looked for a wedding ring. He wasn't wearing one, but of course that meant little. He cleared his throat and began.

"It's true that Claude was smart, and talented,

and handsome. He was probably the most hand-some man any of us have ever seen. But more than that, he was beautiful in the way that we were all beautiful when we were eighteen years old. That's how old we were when we were randomly assigned to be freshman roommates. We were fast friends, and that night in the cafe-teria we met a girl together. We became insepara-ble, the three of us.

"At the very beginning, we thought we were being clever, and we buried a time capsule which we dug up four years later. Well, obviously, it was mostly full of hot air. What was best about us didn't exist yet when we buried that box. The good stuff built up over years. They were the best friends I ever had, or ever will have, and those were without a doubt the best years of my life.

"But let's face it: Claude was always a time bomb. Time capsule, time bomb—I didn't even get the connection until this very second."

George paused, scanned the sea of faces, avoided looking at Ada in the front row or her little girl beside her who looked so much like Claude. He swelled with an impulsive under-standing of just what Claude had done, never allowing any of them to get comfortable with what was good. He had stolen Ada. Broken George's heart and, for a while, his spirit. They'd seen each other only once, briefly, in the years since graduation.

George had left the office to walk around the block on a temperate summer afternoon, his head swimming with the project his team was working on. Distracted, he didn't notice Claude at first; but then, suddenly, his old friend and nemesis was standing right in front of him. Claude looked pretty much the same, a little older but no wiser. It all came flooding back. George felt his face tighten, his blood pump. Claude patted his shoulder and said, gently, "Hey, buddy," as if asking for forgiveness.

George breathed out and said, "Wow."

They chatted briefly and superficially. Neither mentioned Ada, or the fact that she and Claude had had a baby, which George had seen on Facebook. Claude asked if George was still working at Google, and he confirmed that he was. George stopped himself on the verge of asking where Claude lived, thinking it would be better if he didn't know. There was paint on Claude's canvas shoes, and so George assumed he was still making art. It had seemed like a ridiculous luxury to

George, but that was his opinion and he kept it to himself.

"Claude, being Claude, had to go and ruin it. I understand now that he didn't mean to hurt me, or anyone else, but that self-destruction goes hand in hand with other-destruction. I wish he hadn't, but he took us all down together—himself, and me, and Ada, and all of you. But he left something beautiful behind. Not to disagree about his talent as an artist, because he was talented, but it seems to me that the legacy that means the most is his daughter, Claudia."

Hearing George say her daughter's name out loud brought Ada a feeling of unanticipated joy. Maybe because it was so close to Claude's name, it seemed to bring them all together again. She wanted to jump up and throw herself at George, with everyone watching, admit her mistake. She squeezed Claudia closer. No, not mistake; how could she even imagine going back in time and changing anything?

Ada felt suddenly nauseous. Her skin grew prickly with sweat. And then, out of nowhere, she was dizzy. The next thing she knew, she was lying on the floor with her head on her mother's lap. Claudia was holding her hand. Her father was offering her a glass of water. When she opened her eyes, the first person she registered with clarity, hovering above her, concerned and familiar, was George.

The vast living room of Harry and Christina Fisher's penthouse had floor-to-ceiling windows along one whole wall. Outside, the city glimmered in the darkening twilight. Deep-cushioned furniture was arranged in several conversation clusters, with a long sofa facing a fireplace. Above the mantel hung the Fishers' prized Monet: a blue and orange painting, water and boats and sky and trees and moon that Ada might not have identified as a work of the great French artist. Presumably, water lilies would have been beyond the reach even of the Fishers. Claude had been named for the artist, and she found, today, that she couldn't bear to look at the painting or even be in the same room with it.

So instead, she parked herself in the dining room, on a row of chairs facing the food. The Fishers' polished walnut table was large enough to seat at least eighteen people, but they'd understood that no one wanted to be paralyzed by forced conversation that wouldn't come. Thus they had catered a buffet that allowed guests to situate themselves anywhere they pleased. Ada was immeasurably grateful for this accommodation to her own blind grief—a term this day had made clear. By evening she had grown numb, and almost, actually, blind. Her peripheral vision felt blanked out, and sometimes dark splotches obliterated whatever was in front of her. If she blinked, her vision returned, but only briefly. George seemed to understand this intuitively, and he sat beside her, looking straight ahead as if they were strangers on a bus, with Claudia perched on his absently bouncing knee.

"I can't believe it's been five years," Ada said, lamely. She didn't know what to say to George, or how to begin, or if they should try. He was close enough that she could smell him, but he smelled different now.

"It doesn't feel like it." What it felt like, to George, was two days after graduation. Sprawled on his parents' couch, emotionally spent, he couldn't understand why Ada had done it. It felt like six months after that, a thin skin forming over his pain. It felt like one year later, two, three, adjusting to his grown-up, calloused heart. It felt like the walls of time caving in, as if being with Ada again had ruptured perspective.

"I know, right?" To Ada, this felt like the first moment after she'd admitted her infidelity to George, still in their caps and gowns, standing apart from the tent where celebratory families were gathered after the ceremony. To this day, she didn't know why she'd come at it that way, like a kamikaze pilot. This felt like that moment of disbelief, before George had registered what she'd told him, when she still had a chance to say, "Just kidding!"

Claudia slid off George's knee, which bounced a few more beats after she was gone. She headed straight for the bowl of fat strawberries with their green crowns still on. Before reaching for one, she glanced back at her mother, who was still talking to that man. She couldn't tell if her mother was looking at her or at something else. Finally she turned to the strawberries and chose the best one. It was very sweet. She used the back of her hand to wipe off the juice that dripped down her chin, worried that her mother would snap at her about getting her dress dirty, but Ada didn't say anything or even seem to notice.

"How did you find out?" Ada asked George.

For a moment, he didn't understand, and then he did. "Facebook. Like everything else."

"Fucking Facebook."

"I couldn't believe it."

Ada nodded. She knew the feeling.

"I went online and found out about today, and here I am."

"Thanks for coming."

"You're sure you're okay with it?"

"You didn't do anything to me, George."

That was true. He hadn't. "I considered not coming. I didn't want to make you uncomfortable."

"I've been uncomfortable for five years!"

They laughed, a quick burst, and then it shriveled into sadness.

She clarified, "Claude and comfort were opposing forces."

"He wasn't about taking it easy," George agreed. It had made Claude fascinating and exciting and, ultimately, dangerous.

"It's really good to see you, actually."

"It's good to see you, too." He almost turned to look at her, but couldn't, yet. "And your daughter! She's great. You're so lucky to have her."

"I am. Yes."

When, he wanted to ask, but wouldn't, when was she conceived, exactly? It could have been graduation day; the math supported it. Or it could have been soon after. Did it matter? George wasn't sure. But finding out, knowing the fact of it, would likely be a mistake he'd regret.

Two weeks after graduation, she would have told him, had he asked. And if he never asked, she'd never inflict it on him. On the balcony of this penthouse, on a warm night, under the stars.

Ada couldn't figure out what she felt about George now. He felt comfortable, and familiar, and easy, and right, and good. She loved him, but it was different. Just different.

"I really am glad you showed up," she said.

"Well. Showing up is what I do."

It always had been. She remembered that about him. It was one of his many strengths.

He said, "You look good."

"Thanks, but—bullshit. I put on like ten pounds when I had her. I look like a mother."

"No, you don't." But she did. Except it suited her. She had an air of maturity that was new. "Do you work?"

She finally looked at him. "Of course I work.

Believe it or not, Random House actually hired me after my internship. I'm an assistant editor, sort of." She was something in the range of a senior editorial assistant on track to, hopefully, someday, becoming an editor. The pay was abysmal, but the work was interesting. Now, she'd have to either beg for a raise or start waitressing part time in addition to her full-time job, which was out of the question since suddenly she was a single mother. She might have to find a new job. She told herself not to think about that yet, and scanned the room for Claudia, whose mouth was pink from strawberries and who had her hand in the bowl fishing for another one. "What are you doing now?" she asked George.

"Still at Google."

"Wow. So we're both still working at the same places."

"Who would have thought it?" Though George had never, in fact, considered leaving Google. It had been a good job from the beginning, he'd had regular promotions and raises, and the work only got more exciting. He had his own office now, and he shared an assistant with two other engineers.

"We live in Bushwick," she offered. "Where

are you?"

Right here, he wanted to say. I have always been right here.

"Twenty-Second Street between Eighth and Ninth."

"Chelsea—wow."

He lived alone in a two-bedroom apartment, but he wasn't going to tell her that, when most of their classmates were still living with roommates or had moved back in with their parents following the financial crash that had somehow missed him. Bushwick wasn't cheap, but now, with Claude gone…George wasn't going to ask her anything about that. It wasn't his business. Obviously she was still close with her parents. Maybe her plan was to take Claudia and move back to Rhode Island.

George said, "I ran into Claude once. On the street. A few years ago."

"He never told me."

"It was weird. Awkward."

"I bet it was. What did you talk about?"

"Nothing, really." He turned to look at her, hoping she would face him, but she didn't. She continued to rest her gaze somewhere in middle space. "Ada, when did he start using heroin?"

Her eyes fell closed; she shook her head. "I don't know. I found out later that he was high the first time…the day we graduated. All those nights he'd hide out in his studio, painting? He kept his stash there. He'd wait until everyone left and then he'd—"

Her sentence fell off suddenly, into an oblivion of clarity. George could picture it: and then he'd shoot up, alone in the studio, when his friends were studying at the library or making love in Ada's room or grabbing something to eat at the Pub. And they never knew.

"What would we have done, if—?" he began.

"Don't." She cut him off. "Do not go there, okay? The first thing you learn at Nar-Anon is not to blame yourself, and the second thing is that you can't make them stop. Nothing works. You just drive yourself crazy."

"Bounce me!" Claudia was back. George felt a rush of happiness, and lifted her to his knee.

There were no streetlights on McKibbin Street, just a glow spilling from the loft windows. Ada's and Claudia's footsteps clacked along the sidewalk as they hurried past a heap of black garbage bags awaiting morning pickup. It was late, and Claudia was tired, but she refused to be carried. All day long, everyone had told her what a big girl she was now, and she was, and she could walk on her own even this much past her bedtime. But on the way up in the freight elevator, which they weren't really supposed to use, she allowed all her weight to buckle against her mother's legs and felt the relief of surrender. She missed her daddy, but she was about to go to sleep and, if the promise was true, she would see him there.

Ada loved the feel of Claudia's warm, sticky breath on her neck when she carried her into the pink bedroom and lay her carefully down, mouth stained by strawberry juice and still wearing her navy dress. Ada felt so moved by her little girl's peaceful innocence that she started to cry. She pressed the heels of her hands into her eyes to stop herself, removed Claudia's patent leather shoes, and pulled up the covers.

Leaving Claudia's door open an inch, Ada turned on the overhead fluorescents and every lamp until the loft was unforgivingly bright. She sat on the couch and stared into the large space. Three days ago, when the call had come from the emergency room nurse, Claudia had been sitting on the floor with a stack of paper and a box of crayons. She had drawn three peanut shapes with stick arms and stick legs, and had started to apply scribbles that passed for hair, when Ada yanked her up by the armpits and hauled her to the hospital.

Claude had been found in Central Park, at the foot of the Alice in Wonderland statue, already dead. He'd once told her that he'd loved playing there as a boy. She assumed it was deliberate, shooting up beside the statue. Deliberate and macabre. How dare he?

Now, Claudia's drawing and crayons sat exactly where they'd been hastily abandoned. A pair of Claude's blue socks was still clumped under the table where they ate their meals. His black zippered sweater was draped over a chair. The Junot Díaz novel he'd been reading was splayed facedown on the coffee table. Four nights ago he'd left it there, saying he had to go find a bookmark, and then got distracted by something else.

Ada picked up the book and threw it across the room, shattering a water glass that had been sitting out since she-couldn't-remember-when.

She kicked off her shoes, stretched her legs out on the couch, and waited for either sleep or morning.

George walked and walked, trying to clear his mind. He'd forgotten his gloves, and his fingertips were frozen. He stopped in a deli for some coffee. Standing on the avenue, late, people hurrying home, he cupped his hands around the hot cardboard cup and inhaled the steam that rose from the notch in the plastic cover. The coffee was acrid and weak, but he didn't care. What he wanted was its warmth, on his hands, in his throat. Seeing Ada had upset him. But skipping Claude's funeral had not been an option.

Standing there, in the flow of evening, he thought of a poem Ada had recited to him and Claude in the cafeteria one dinnertime. She was writing a paper on obscure Victorian verse and had insisted they hear one that, she'd said, reminded her of "us, right now." Years later, he'd found it in an online search of the phrase "the beautiful years," the one thing about the poem that had stayed with him. He found it easily, and memorized it so that he could listen to it in his mind, as often as he wanted to, spoken in Ada's voice:

*Eheu! Fugaces, by A. Eubule Evans*

*I've seen them again*
*As the Dream stood by—*
*The beautiful years*
*I once let die.*

*As the Dream stood by,*
*He whispered a word,*
*And the beautiful years*
*Once more appeared.*

*He whispered a word;*
*And its sound in truth*
*Was strong as a spell;*
*For that word was "Youth."*

*"O beautiful years,"*
*I eagerly cried,*
*"You will stay here now!"*
*But no voice replied.*

*And I saw them fade*

*Away through my tears—*
*They were dreams themselves,*
*Those beautiful years.*

The coffee lost its heat, and he dropped it, nearly full, into a mesh trash can on the corner of 53rd and Lexington. He took his phone out of his pocket and stared at it. All the pretty apps stared back at him. He hated that Claude was dead. Their denouement had been so fully unanticipated that they'd never said goodbye at graduation; after Ada's confession, George escaped with his parents, and that was that. Even after their chance meeting in the street that time, nothing was definitive. George had always assumed that somehow, one day, they would all come to understand each other; that they would find a way to look back and make sense of what had happened. But now, Claude's death fixed them in place. *Make art, kill love, die young* could have been carved onto his tombstone and it wouldn't be too wrong, too harsh or too brief.

George wondered where Claude would be buried. Or if he'd be buried. Ashes stored in an urn on the mantel beneath the Monet? Ashes scattered somewhere? It didn't matter where

Claude's remains ended up, because it was true, true, that when you loved someone, they lived on in memory.

Claude lying on his narrow college bed, stretched long, elbows winged behind his head. Thinking.

Claude dancing in the Slonim common room, sweating. Red and orange strobe lights freezing him in variants of movement.

Claude cutting the fat off the edge of his pork chop.

Claude filling a basket at Pearl Paint on Canal Street.

Claude starting to tug the old tape off the time capsule. "Here we go!"

And Ada, always, always with them in the memory. Ada, who had belonged to George. Ada.

George swiped open his contacts, wondering if Beth was available. She answered after four rings, as if she'd considered letting it slide to voice mail and then decided, what the hell.

"Hey."

"Hey. Can I come over?"

"Right now?"

"I was just at a funeral, a friend from college."

"Aw, baby. Doorbell's broken. Text when

you're outside and I'll buzz you in."

She was a graduate student at Parsons, they'd met at a party a few months ago, and she lived in a shitty part of midtown that realtors were now calling "the garment district." From her bedroom window you could see the long, curving ramp the buses took out of Port Authority.

When he got there, she was halfway through an episode of Game of Thrones. He watched the rest with her, reclined on her couch, holding hands. Then they went to her bed and had sex. After, he lay beside her, naked under a top sheet. They didn't touch.

When they'd met, they were both drunk and she'd said, "I bet you're good in the feathers—I read that Ava Gardner said that about Frank Sinatra." She was funny, and pretty, and they'd screwed twice that first night. They'd never been out to dinner, but they'd slept together half a dozen times, always at her apartment. A strand of her long brown hair rested on his shoulder, and he looked at her. Smiled, in gratitude.

"Are you hungry?" she asked. "I could make something."

She'd fed him before, and she was a good cook. And he thought, Why not?

## BEGIN AGAIN

The day before, thinking he was helping, George had spent over an hour pulling clumps of weeds out of the beach. The feeling of cleaning up, smoothing surfaces, was intensely satisfying, as if he could rip ugly tangles of error out of his path, toss them away, move forward. Then, one of the tent installers had informed him that the grasses helped anchor the sand; without them, over time, the beach would erode into the pond. George had apologized—not that it was the tent guy's beach, but even so. Having grown up in the city, George knew practically nothing about the details of ecosystems.

Now, in his tuxedo, the tent billowing white in

the adjacent grove of trees, George stood alone on the beach, admiring its imperfections. Nature was funny that way: how, the older you got, the more it became a mirror reflecting back elements of your evolving self. Wisdom in a mayhem of roots, sand, ripples on the ever-changing surface of water. He felt like laughing at himself—at all the stupid assumptions and raw hopes that had propelled him to here, today, this beach—but didn't. There was still a lot to do, and he'd developed a tic-like apprehension that something could go terribly wrong at the eleventh hour.

The caterers had arrived and were setting up the tables. Seventy-five guests were expected. They had wanted to keep it as small as possible, but the list had quickly grown from forty. Overall, their philosophy had been to hurt no one's feelings; thus, if an ancient aunt from the margins of one of their families would feel left out, she'd receive an invitation. Everything was kept simple. No passed hors d'oeuvres. A buffet. Just wine and beer. Friends would take pictures and videos. A trio of classical string musicians from a local college. George's only regrets, and they were minor, were not hiring a professional photographer and that the cake was too small. The weather was perfect, seventy-seven degrees, a few light clouds hanging in a clear blue sky. The periphery of the vast pond was edged in houses, mostly summer homes. A single fishing boat floated in the distance.

An earthy smell of marijuana drifted over, and he was transported back to college. To Claude, and Ada, and the irreplaceable lost friendship of those years. They'd smoked a lot of pot, Claude especially, the thought of which dropped like a weight on George's mood. Had Claude lived, if things had gone differently, he'd be the best man today. Instead, it was going to be George's younger brother, John.

John, who, at fifteen, was the only one George could think of who would consider it an acceptable idea to get stoned an hour before the wedding. George walked through the brush, past where the jetty extended into the pond, and there was his brother in his good suit, hair shaggy, suddenly tall and bursting with hormones, sucking on the end of a twisted white joint.

"You've got to be fucking kidding me," George said.

John faced him, pimply, serene. "Cheers, brother. You want some?"

"No, thanks. I hope you have some drops—I don't really want to see those bloodshot eyes next to me at the altar." Not that there was to be an actual altar, but he'd made his point.

"Yup, all set. No worries." John smiled. "You look awesome, dude."

"Thanks. So do you."

"Ready for this?"

"Definitely." George had been ready for a long time. He had recently turned thirty. He was still working at Google, and he had more employees and was making more money than he had ever imagined. Still, he had started to feel that what he'd really wanted from his life had passed him by. That it was almost too late. And then, suddenly, it wasn't.

Twenty-three satin buttons climbed the back of Ada's dress. She'd bought it at a thrift store on Thompson Street, and with tailoring the whole thing had run less than two hundred dollars. They'd spent three times that on their rings, but they'd agreed that they prioritized correctly. Ada had insisted on paying for her own dress, along with the flowers and the cake. She'd been able to make ends meet these past two years with extra income that Jacka Tornado had generated from sales of Claude's work. And she was an editor now, with a small raise that had allowed her to feel that she'd finally grasped the far edge of adulthood. Nothing was anything like what she'd expected a decade ago when they were in school; she had never imagined the land mines buried in life's choices. Later, she would look back at herself as a bride and recognize how young she was on that beautiful summer day, how much there was yet to learn about love and family and life. She was, today, nearly thirty years old and felt mature. Steady. Prepared. In other words, ready enough to proceed.

"Hold still," Lori ordered her sister, who kept twisting to check on the progress of the buttons. "It's tight. There's no give. When you move, I can't get the button into the hole."

"Sorry."

George's sister Ellen, heavily pregnant, about to pop, said, "I can't imagine ever being thin enough to fit into my wedding gown again."

"You will be," Ada assured her. Though Ada, having done things backward—baby first, marriage later—suspected that this dress would have sagged on her younger self. She didn't care. Of all the things they'd fussed over these past months—the details of the ceremony, the clothes, the food—what mattered to her was that she'd ended up where she should have started. With George. Though sometimes, even now, a mist of Claude hung between them. Years ago, on graduation day, she'd been unwilling to believe in anything more powerful than the immediate moment. The fabric of her striped dress peeling away. The feel of his tongue curling around hers. She emptied her lungs so Ellen could secure the buttons running up her ribs.

Claudia, now a lanky seven-year-old, stood by the bed in Ada's childhood room, wearing a pretty dress she had chosen herself: white lace over pink satin, with a tiny bow at her neck. Her brown hair, dark and thick like her father's, waved past her shoulders. More and more, she grew a startling resemblance to Claude: his riveting beauty, his scowl, his lit-up eyes, his love of risk. But she had Ada in her, too: the freckle-dusted cheeks, long legs and broad shoulders, forgiveness, humor. Some days Ada even imagined that she saw George there—the quiet thoughtfulness and easy smile. Ada looked at her daughter and corrected her thinking. Claudia was all of them and none of them; she was herself.

Claudia stood very still. She'd been admonished earlier not to ruin her dress, an order so broad as to worry her that any move could be disastrous. She held her basket of rose petals, ready to go, though the procession wouldn't begin for nearly an hour. She was very happy today. She adored George. When her mother had explained that he was her first love, she didn't quite understand, because in the same conversation her own father, Claude, had been Ada's true love. First and true seemed like the same thing to Claudia. She'd noticed that, whenever she did something for the first time, it felt the most real, and real was true. Her mother had said that it was hard to explain, which was the only part of the conversation that had made perfect sense, since it was equally hard to comprehend. When Ada had tried to clarify that she, George and Claude had once been best friends all together, Claudia began to get the idea. She had a best friend at school, a girl, and there was a boy they often played with. The boy seemed equally happy to spend time with either girl. Maybe that was how Ada felt about George and

Claude. She had promised that, one day, Claudia would understand.

Ada hadn't seen either of her parents for much of the morning; hosting the wedding at their house was keeping them occupied. She could hear Diana's voice downstairs, supervising someone. Deliveries had been coming all day. Guests were starting to arrive. From the bedroom window, Ada watched Philip, in the same suit he'd worn to her college graduation, helping his elderly mother down the grassy slope toward the beach. Ellen's husband Kenji appeared next, carrying a tray of empty wine glasses. Ada laughed, seeing that.

"Look at Ken."

Ellen and Lori glanced out the window, and Ellen said, "He can't sit still, that man."

Ada said, "I think it's nice." She had grown used to Kenji's cheerful restlessness.

There was a knock on the door. "Can I come in? It's Missy."

"Entrée," Lori said.

George's mother held a charm bracelet in her hand, with a pearl necklace draped over her wrist. She'd been generous throughout, but Ada worried; Missy had seemed to forgive too easily the betrayal of her son. Ada smiled at the older woman who, in hours, would be her mother-in-law. She had promised to share something borrowed, and had evidently brought two options. The dress was old. The shoes were new. And Ada was wearing a pair of blue silk panties. What she lacked was the sixpence-in-her-shoe piece of the old tradition—the part signifying prosperity. They already had that, thanks to George, and it was the aspect she cared least about. Somehow, Claude's wealth had poisoned him; or maybe it was his parents' application of that wealth to his childhood. Through knowing him, Ada had learned not to misinterpret the promise of money.

"How about both?" Ada asked.

Missy smiled. "I was hoping you'd say that." She came around to clasp the pearl necklace around Ada's neck. "This belonged to my mother. I wore it on my wedding day."

Ada was touched. "Thank you."

"And this," now, attaching the charm bracelet to Ada's right wrist, "belongs to all of us. It was my great-grandmother's, and every time someone gets married, it gets a new charm."

"You wear it until your first anniversary," Ellen explained. "Not all the time, just whenever you feel like it. Then it gets put away until the next wedding in the family."

"Will I get one?" Claudia asked, still frozen in her spot. She liked the way the charms dangled and clanked off the bracelet's chain. Hers would be a key, because she loved secrets. Or a cupcake. Or a kitten. She wasn't sure.

Ada's pulse quickened. What if Claudia were left out of the family tradition? She wasn't, after all, George's biological child. She glanced at Missy, who said, "Of course you will!"

Relieved, Ada raised her wrist to eye level. There were seven charms: a milk bottle, a hoe, a horse, a book, a flower, a heart, and a hammer. "Which is mine, the book?"

"No. The husband-to-be chooses it."

"The heart?"

Missy nodded. "George picked it out eight years ago."

Ada was shocked. She looked at the dime-size silver heart. "Eight years?"

"Didn't he tell you?" Missy was upset with herself; she had spoken out of school. George and Ada's relationship hadn't followed a straight line. She shouldn't have assumed, well, anything. All she knew was that, about a month before graduation, George had asked her to go shopping with him one weekend when he was home visiting from college. He'd said he needed a charm, for Ada, and Missy understood what that meant. The next thing she knew, they had broken up, and Ada had gone with her son's best friend. Why hadn't George told her that Ada still didn't know about his intention to propose on graduation day? If he kept her in the dark, how would she be able to protect him from this young woman with her unpredictable appetites? Missy forced herself not to think about that now. It was her son's wedding day, and she was here to celebrate. And later, once their vows were taken, to give the newlyweds something that she suspected George had forgotten all about: a letter he wrote when he was six and sealed into an envelope which he marked in thick red crayon, for mi weding day. She had waited twenty-four years to deliver it.

Until earlier that year, George had never mentioned anything to Ada about marriage. Certainly not when they were students. Ada now wondered if Claude had known, and her skin prickled. He'd told her that he had "lusted after her since day one." George and Claude had been roommates, and they'd been very close. How could Claude not have known?

"That's sweet," Ada said, recovering.

"Isn't it? I'm the hammer." Ellen was an architect. "Gigi, our great-grandmother, started the tradition. She was the hoe."

Ada, Lori and Ellen burst out laughing. Even Claudia joined in. Missy looked mystified and pretended not to understand.

Claudia came first, handfuls of white petals preceding her on the mossy, root-veined ground. Her pulse raced when she came around the hump that separated the grove from the beach and saw so many people watching her. People were taking pictures, and she liked it. She wanted to smile but thought better of it and told herself, one handful at a time, toss them higher and they'll float before they land.

Lori came next, stepping, and pausing, and stepping, careful to re-set the rhythm for the processional since Claudia had charmingly forgotten the instructions.

Ellen concentrated on her balance, afraid

she'd topple over. Her water had broken just before the music started, but she wanted to get through this before alerting Kenji that they'd have to duck out and find the nearest hospital. The baby was three weeks early. The insides of her legs were wet, but, luckily, the dress was long enough and loose enough to hide it.

Ada followed slowly between Diana and Philip, her arms linked with theirs. The last time they had walked this way had been at Claude's funeral, and her parents had practically been holding her up; but she didn't want to think about that, not today. George stood on the beach between his brother, John, and the justice of the peace—a woman with short blonde hair wearing a turquoise robe, whom they had met only once before—smiling with his eyes while his lips clenched back emotion. He looked like he was on the verge of crying, and she wanted to run to him, but she held her pace. He was so handsome, her George, so loving and kind. As she neared, she remembered the very first time she saw him: on the evening of the first day of orientation, in the cafeteria, standing on line for a hot dog, when by chance she stood behind him and in front of Claude. She remembered thinking that she couldn't decide which boy was cuter, that they were both beautiful but in different ways, and that college was going to be a blast.

George had been the first to speak to her—staying in character, as she would eventually learn. When they'd reached the food, he picked up an extra paper plate and turned around to hand it to her, saying, "Here you go."

"Thanks," she'd answered, taken off guard by his courtesy.

"Where are you from?"

"Rhode Island."

"I'm from Queens."

At the time, she'd known nothing about the city; the difference between Queens and Brooklyn or any other borough would have been, to her, a layman's comparison of distant stars. "Oh," she'd said, as he stepped forward and extended his plate to the obese woman in a hair net who was serving the food. Ada hadn't consciously registered the server's face—she was just some fat lady—but now, suddenly, as she walked toward George in her wedding gown, as he stood there brimming with emotion, as behind him in the distance a fisherman paused to watch, she recalled the woman with clarity. Her expression was full of passive mockery. The entitled freshmen, awaiting their dinner, unseeing.

George watched his Ada, who'd made the fearless choice of a pure white gown, but a gown without veil or train. No pretense, no past. She walked toward him, slowly, slowly, and he could see her thinking about something and wondered what it was. His mind was full of her. With John, Ellen, Lori and Claudia now at his side, and the justice of the peace patiently waiting, Ada was the last to arrive. By the time she was beside him, he felt as if a hundred years had passed.

Philip stood on the beach, feeling gray and happy, and watched his oldest daughter promise her future to George. He and Diana had known this man since he was a teenager, and trusted him, implicitly. He recalled the first time Ada had brought George home, that long-ago Thanksgiving, the three college students weaving their newfound intellectualism into the conversation at the table, both young men clearly smitten with his daughter, but never a forewarning of how their paths would collide with such fury. A face from Philip's own past swam into his consciousness: his own first love, Kathy, in 1979, green eyes bright with misdirection, smiling when she told him she was going home for the weekend for her aunt's birthday, when in fact she had scheduled an abortion. He'd never even known she was pregnant, until she mentioned it later with an underlying attitude of de facto what's-done-is-done that ruined their chances of moving forward together. It had been her right, but it had ruined trust. He didn't understand women, not even after thirty-two years of marriage to Diana; but he had learned through trial and error to suspend judgment, and that skill had seen him through.

Beside Philip, Diana floated on the blissful moment when everything was done, taken care of, the party was underway and now whatever happened would be the story. How lucky her daughter was for this chance at a rewrite. She thought that George's brother's eyes looked a little bloodshot, standing beside the groom, and wondered if the mattress of the pullout bed she'd put him on needed to be replaced.

Harry could practically smell it on his teenage son from all the way over here, clumped on the beach with the other guests, facing the ceremony and the pond. But John was his third child, and Harry knew enough not to let it matter too much. George had finally got his girl, and Harry dismissed any inkling of emotion, today, except triumph.

Missy clutched her pale yellow handbag, eager for the ceremony to end, waiting for her chance to hand over the sealed envelope. She still hadn't decided whom, exactly, she was supposed to give it to, George or Ada. For my wedding day was all it said; or, rather, for mi weding day. Every time she thought of that, she had to suppress a bubble of mirth. What, she now wondered, did she want the note to say? Should she have ripped it open and slipped in her own message? How dare you hurt my son.

Claudia sat between Ada and George at the big round family table in the middle of the tent, sharing a single piece of cake. She'd wanted her own but had been told that it wasn't quite big enough for everyone and so they'd have to share.

"It's a metaphor," Ada said, and smiled a clever smile, but it only made Claudia mad. It wasn't that thing, a metta-4, it was a piece of cake. She hated it when her mother said things she couldn't decipher.

Ada looked at George and appreciated the way he smiled and said, "Exactly." Secretly, though, he looked forward to the day when things between them would carry less weight, and just be what they were.

Claudia hunkered between and beneath their secret talk, growing even madder. Now, was it two against one? She pulled the cake plate closer to her and dug in without regard to either of them. They said nothing about it. She finished the cake herself.

And then a warm, wine-smelling voice spoke from above. Claudia looked up, and there was George's mother, whom she was supposed to call Grandma now, giving her three grandmothers in all. It would mean more presents at birthdays and holidays, and so she decided it made her lucky.

"I have something for you," Grandma Missy said. Claudia twisted around to see a white envelope being offered.

George threw his head back, laughing, and said, "Oh, wow. I forgot all about that!" He couldn't remember what he wrote when he was a little boy, but he had a vague memory of handing it to his mother while she cooked dinner in the kitchen. Her apron was orange striped. The smell was of baking chicken and sweet potatoes. He remembered, now, that she'd patted his head, slipped the envelope into a kitchen drawer, and returned to meal preparations.

"What is it?" Ada recognized the tilted chunky lettering of a very young child. Claudia had only recently evolved beyond that wild early penmanship. "Did you write that?" she asked George. Another time capsule, even more distant than the first one. "Can I see?" But before Missy could put the envelope into Ada's hand, Claudia reached up to snatch it.

Claudia said, "I want to open it." The grown-ups all stared at her, a little bit startled, but she didn't care. She ripped the end off the envelope and then gutted it to retrieve the small, folded paper inside. She knew how to read, basically, but this was ridiculous. She announced, "Someone can't spell."

Ada leaned over her daughter. The note said, yu cen hav al mi jelybens. She looked at George, who was also reading the note. She kissed the soft skin behind his ear and whispered, "I have to ask you something."

"What?"

She lifted her wrist, touched the silver heart.

"Did you get this for me when we were still in college?"

"Yes."

"Did Claude know?"

He nodded, and saw something shift in her eyes. "I'm sorry, I didn't want to bring all that up when things were going so well with us, I—"

"You don't have to explain." Her voice, gentle, stopped him. It was Claude who needed to explain how he could do that to his best friend, aware of George's intentions, but it would never happen and they would both have to live with that. "I was an idiot," she shook the letter, "when I could have had all of your jellybeans all this fucking time."

As their gaze met above Claudia's head, they laughed nervously and pivoted together into a kiss. A kiss, for Ada, that was a deliverance. For George, a reprieve.

Claudia wiggled out from under them. She didn't understand what they were discussing, but something about it introduced a sharp disappointment into her mood. She looked at her empty plate, hazed with white frosting, and suddenly didn't care if there wasn't enough cake for everyone. She wanted more. One day, when she was a teenager, she would remember this as a moment of recognition: there was a dullness in her mother, an aversion to the kind of risk the little girl already hungered for; an understanding that Ada would blunt the raw promise of her daughter's future; the planting of a seed of resentment that would eventually replace gratitude as the guiding force of her adolescence. She would spend an entire night searching the internet for who her father really was and, failing to find more than the blabbering of art critics, would commit herself to emulating him by reinvention. She would become the beautiful flare of him that hadn't survived his own impulses. And then, like her mother, she would learn that urges extinguish themselves over time. Like any child, she would discover herself only after devouring both her parents, and spend her waning years toggling between restlessness and satisfaction. She slid off her chair.

"Where are you going?" Ada's voice followed her, but she didn't turn around.

Across the tent, Claudia saw a sliver of cake left where the whole towering confection was before, and hurried to get there first.

# ACKNOWLEDGMENTS

A writer without editors or readers is a lonely soul. And so I am grateful to editor Alison Castleman for her intelligence, sensitivity and keen ear for language, and to copy editor Joseph McCombs for his eagle-sharp eyes. And to both Karenna Lief and Oliver Lief for being this novella's first readers; your enthusiasm reassured me that following the strong feeling that led to this work was, if nothing else, a good use of my time

# ABOUT THE AUTHOR

Katia Lief is the international bestselling author of crime novels and other fiction. She teaches creative writing at The New School in Manhattan and lives with her family in Brooklyn.

 facebook.com/readkatialief

 twitter.com/KatiaLief

 instagram.com/katia.lief

www.ingramcontent.com/pod-product-compliance
Lightning Source LLC
Chambersburg PA
CBHW032010120726
47902CB00014B/2072